Little
HORRORS

Shiver with fear...

Owwl!

...shake with laughter!

For Tom and Will

Visit Shoo Rayner's website!
www.shoo-rayner.co.uk

ORCHARD BOOKS
96 Leonard Street, London EC2A 4XD
Orchard Books Australia
Unit 31/56 O'Riordan Street, Alexandria, NSW 2015
First published in Great Britain in 2001
First paperback edition 2002
Copyright © Shoo Rayner 2001
The right of Shoo Rayner to be identified as the author
and illustrator of this work has been asserted by him in
accordance with the Copyright, Designs, and Patents Act, 1988.
A CIP catalogue record for this book is available
from the British Library.
ISBN 1 84121 638 0 (hardback)
ISBN 1 84121 646 1 (paperback)
1 3 5 7 9 10 8 6 4 2 (hardback)
3 5 7 9 10 8 6 4   (paperback)
Printed in Great Britain

Little

HORRORS

The Swamp Man

ShooRayner

ORCHARD BOOKS

I couldn't bear to look.
It was just too horrible…

5

Mum and Dad were being all
soppy and lovey-dovey. My sister,
Kim, and I were nearly sick!

Mum and Dad were going away
for a romantic weekend. And *we*
were going to stay with Aunt Loopy.

Aunt Loopy's name suits her. She
really *is* quite loopy!

Mum and Dad gave us
the usual talk.

Why do parents make such a fuss? If they're going, why can't they just go?

As they drove away, Aunt Loopy got all excited. "Ooh! We're going to have fun this weekend. I've got a special surprise planned for tonight!"

We couldn't wait. Aunt Loopy's surprises were always fun.

We decided to spend the afternoon exploring.

A winding path led from the front gate, round the house, and down to the bottom of the garden.

It was brilliant for skateboarding!

At the end of the path we made
a ramp from an old plank of wood.
If you went fast enough, you could
jump right over the pond.

Go too slowly though, and you'd land right in it. *Yuck!* No thank you! The pond was covered in duckweed and slimy, slippery, stinky sludge.

Kim and I skateboarded all afternoon. It was quite dangerous, because Aunt Loopy's dog, Treacle, kept leaping out of the bushes and attacking the skateboard!

Itchy, Scratchy and Nits sat
together in the shadows. Their big
green eyes followed our every move.

It was nearly dark when Aunt
Loopy called us inside.
Was it time for our big surprise?

Aunt Loopy was holding a big bowl of popcorn.

"My big surprise is coming later," she said, excitedly. "Let's watch a film while we wait. It'll be a scream!"

We turned the lights off and put the tape in the video. It was called...

...*The Swamp Man.*
The music was really creepy.

But Aunt Loopy cackled like a crazy old witch! She thought it was the funniest thing ever.

Kim and I didn't. We watched from behind the sofa.

A noise outside made me jump.

Treacle heard it too.
She sat up, ears pricked.

20

Aunt Loopy twitched the curtain
and peered out of the window.

The music got louder and louder…

…and the screen went green.

The Swamp Man was dripping
in gooey slime. It raised its horrid,
yellow, rotting face and groaned.

A loud groan echoed from outside. Then a strange, low, rumbling noise shook the house.

Something was out there!

Treacle barked.

Kim looked terrified.
She zapped the remote control
and the video snapped off.

The rumbling sound circled round
the house. Treacle began howling.
The *something* started wailing.

Three loud bangs from the kitchen made us jump.

Could it be the Swamp Man?

No, it was Itchy, Scratchy and Nits tearing through the catflap.

Hissing and spitting, they leapt onto the back of the sofa. The fur was bristling on their backs.

Treacle barked even louder.

Then, everything stopped.
We held our breath. The silence
surrounded us like a bubble.

Suddenly, it burst with a blood-curdling scream, followed by a tremendous splash.

Then, soft, squelchy footsteps
dragged around the side of the house.
Treacle whimpered.

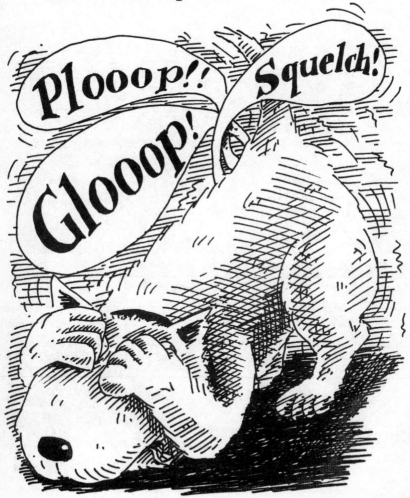

Through a gap in the curtain we saw a hideous shape lurch towards the front door.

Slowly...ever so slowly... it raised an arm...

...and rang the doorbell.

33

Treacle howled. The cats wauled.

The *something* spoke in a desperate, watery voice.

"Don't be ridiculous," said Aunt Loopy. "There's no such thing."

She marched up to the door, opened it and…screamed!

The Swamp Man was standing
on the doorstep!

He was covered in revolting green
slime and had a horrid, yellow,
rotting face.

Treacle hurled herself at him.

She ripped a lump of yellow goo
from his face and...and...

...ate it!

"Hey, gerroff!" complained the Swamp Man.

Treacle tore the rest of the goo from the Swamp Man's face.

"Paul!" cried Aunt Loopy. "Oh, you poor thing. What happened to you?"

She turned to us.

"This is Paul. *He's* my special surprise! We're going to get married. He was bringing some pizza for a treat!"

This is what had happened…
I'd left the skateboard by the gate.

Paul had stepped on it…

…whooshed down to the bottom
of the garden…

Wooah!

Woooosh!

...up the ramp...

...over the rockery - and into the green, slimy pond.

On the way, the pizza had ended up on top of his head!

Paul smiled. He gazed into Aunt Loopy's eyes.

"Never mind, dearest. I'm really quite all right."

Aunt Loopy sighed and gave him a squelchy hug.

Paul went home to get changed.
Very soon he was back with
fresh pizzas. They were delicious.

While we ate, Paul gave something to Aunt Loopy.

He spoke to her in a dreamy voice, as though we weren't even there.

It was a videotape. A man and a woman were kissing on the cover. It was called…

…True Romance.

Kim and I looked at each other.

"A soppy movie!" we screamed.
"No way are we watching that!
We'll have nightmares all week!"